THE ADVENTURES OF SWEARLOT HOLMES

Excerpts from his most thrilling adventures

Collated by Earle Wilkinson

Paperback ISBN 978-1-78092-879-1
ePub ISBN 978-1-78092-880-7
PDF ISBN 978-1-78092-881-4

Published in the UK by MX Publishing
335 Princess Park Manor, Royal Drive, London, N11 3GX
www.mxpublishing.com

Dedicated to my most wonderful good lady Joanne Kitching.
Dean Earle Wilkinson, 2015

'My name is Swearlot Holmes and it is my fucking
business to know what other fucking people don't.
Fart that on your fat wife's tits.'

Illustrated by Sidney Paget, Frank Wiles, Howard E.Elcock & Ruby Kitching. Cover design by Graeme Wilkinson, 6E Creative www.6e.net
With thanks to The Baker Street Twats: Brenda Littler, Mark Robertson, Gillie Hatton, Martin Casson & Brian Littler

ABOUT THE AUTHOR

Dean (Earle) Wilkinson is a television scriptwriter, novelist and games writer. He was Ant and Dec's writer for seven years penning the multi-award winning SMTV Live & Chums. He penned two series of his own CBBC sitcom Bad Penny starring Graham Fellows (aka comedian John Shuttleworth), as well as two series of his sketch show Stupid starring Marcus Brigstock and Phil Cornwell. As a games writer, he has written for the entire LittleBigPlanet series, Fantasia: Music Evolved, Driver San Francisco and Worms, amongst many many others.

His long writing career has seen him scribbling for Stephen Fry, Hugh Laurie, John Cleese, Smith & Jones, Matt Berry, Brian Conley, Noel Edmonds, Chris Barry, Zig & Zag, The Krankies, Simon Pegg and Harry Hill to name drop but a few.

Dean is father to three daughters, Emily, Alice and Grace. He writes adult comedy as Earle Wilkinson and kid's / family comedy as Dean Wilkinson.

www.deanwilkinson.net

BOOKS AS DEAN WILKINSON

The SMTV Live Annual
The Legend Of Arthur King
Arthur King & The Curious Case Of The Time Train
The Classic Children's Television Quiz Book
Sarkylocks & The Three Bears
The Greenies: A Mountain Of Trouble
The Plants Versus Zombies Book Of Things To Do Quiz Book
The Beano Prankipedia
Sheerluck's 7 Mysteriously Mysterious Mysteries Volume 1

EXCERPTS

Foreword by Dr John Watson

So appalled was I whilst re-reading my encounters with the world's first swearing detective, Mr Swearlot Holmes, that I was moved to throw them in the fire. It was a silly idea as the fire was not, at that time, lit.

That I had to aurally witness his foul-mouthed transgressions was indeed terrible enough, but the fact I actually wrote them down in the first person beggars belief! What was I thinking!

But, to my abject shame I did just that. I vow the original transcripts will never see the light of day.

However, my own biographer, Mr Wilkinson, offered to rewrite these stories in story form so my shame might be saved by some small degree. He said I owed it to history, literature and the Science Of Swearing And Obscene Gestures that I let him do so. I was deeply unsure, but when he showed me the advance salary from the publishers, I was moved to concede.

These are but a handful of our adventures punctuated by my dear friend's reprehensible tongue. I ask only one thing as you peruse them: do not let them be seen by the young, the prudish or the frail of mind. And indeed any other bunch of doyles.

Dr John M. Watson, MD.

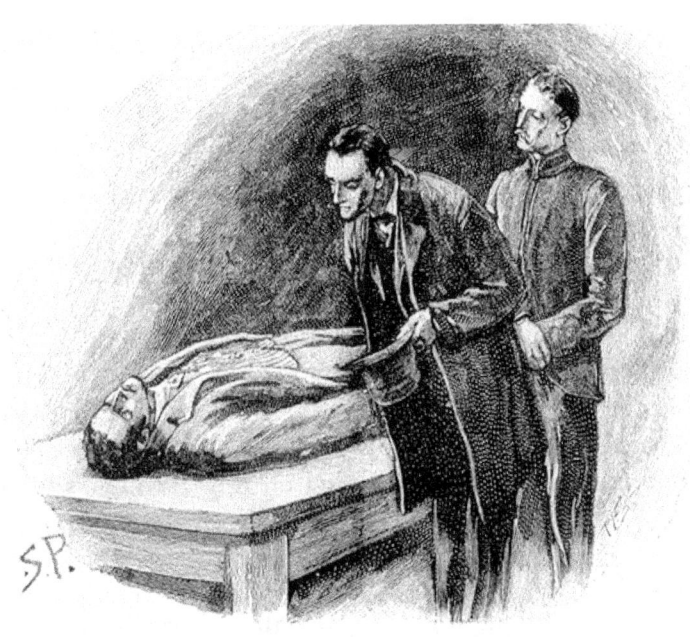

1. THE ADVENTURE OF THE HERRING DERRINGER

The young police officer turned to Swearlot Holmes looking baffled. The consulting detective was examining every inch of the corpse with silent and studied vigour. In particular the bullet wound to the unfortunate man's right temple and the large, plump herring on the fishmonger's floor not a foot away.

'Any idea how Barcrest the fishmonger died, sir?' asked the young constable.

'Isn't it obvious?' replied Holmes. "The bastard's been trampled by a herd of fucking elephants.'

The constable's eyes widened. 'Elephants? But... but...' he stammered.

'Of course not, you thick prick. Now sod off lest I punch you in the ball bag,' snapped Holmes without looking up. Adding '*Wanker*' as the fellow made his retreat.

He almost barged Watson off his feet in his haste as the good Doctor strolled in through the shop doorway.

'What's his problem?' asked Watson.

'He's got a stick of dynamite up his arsehole that he wants to crap out before it goes off,' replied Holmes.

'Good Lord, how on Earth did it get up there?' Watson looked quite dazed with concern.

Holmes narrowed his eyes to Watson and tilted his head.

'Fucking seriously?' growled Holmes. 'If you're going to be dafter than a fart in a fucking trance, you can piss right off now.'

A pregnant pause gave birth to an uneasy moment of silence. Both Holmes and Watson examined the corpse.

'What do you think killed him?' Watson finally asked.

Before he'd uttered the final word Holmes had punched him in the ball bag.

......

From 'The Adventure Of The Mysterious
Turd In The Persian Slipper.'

Holmes puffed his pipe then said, 'No I sent Inspector Leturd
instead. Don't take this the wrong way, Watson, but you
couldn't find your own arse with both hands and a fucking
compass.'

From 'A Study In Brown Ale.'

'But Mr Holmes, the corpse is behind you,' said Fortherskill.
'Seriously?' replied Holmes, 'Sorry, I'm pissed out of
my fucking head.'

From 'The Adventure Of The Hourly Rates.'

'We'll find your missing wife once we have played hide and seek,' snapped Holmes, 'Now start fucking counting!'

2. THE MESSAGE OF THE DOGS' BOLLOCKS

Holmes eyed the testicles carefully.

'You'll be glad to know, gentlemen, that no hound suffered by the removal of these gonads. It was done with expert surgery. A vet of the highest proficiency removed these as part of painless neutering operations.'

'Operations?' queried Watson. 'Plural. You think they are from two separate dogs?'

'Indubitably. They are of differing size and hair colouring. This canine spud on the left is from an Alsatian and the other once hung between the thighs of a Red Setter.'

'But why send them to Miss Applebottom, Holmes? It defies common sense,' said Inspector Leturd.

'It is a statement as to what might have been.'

'Explain, old fellow,' said Watson blankly.

'Remember Miss Applebottom spoke of her suitor whom she rejected last year? The Jenkins fellow. She said he was too working class for the stuck up bitch. This week I read in the Times that he's now a multi-millionaire after finding success in the gold fields of Australia. These ghoulies are to visually illustrate what her life could have been like if she hadn't been such a prissy arsehole.'

Watson and Leturd both shook their heads, neither of them following the thread. Holmes was amazed as it was so clear and simple to him.

'You really don't know what I'm talking about, do you? It's swearing. My splendid art,' said Holmes incredulously.

Again, no response from the two.

'Dear God. What is it like in your soap-washed little mouths? It must be so boring. If something is awful it's *bollocks*, but if something is wonderful, amazing and exciting it's the *dog's bollocks*. Jenkins is saying her life could've been the dog's bollocks,' said Holmes.

Leturd and Watson both nodded and pulled that face people do when they don't understand something but do not want to admit for fear of looking twats.

'No, don't do that. Seriously. You both look like twats right now. Stop! Stop pulling those faces!' demanded Holmes.

......

SWEARLOT HOLMES

THE ADVENTURE
OF THE
MAN WITH THE DIRTY BOOKS

Professor Morifarty's A Brief History Of Swearing

Flamin' Nora

Originally, this time honoured exclamation of surprise, was *Flaming Horror* originating in London, England. Over the centuries, slack-gobbed Cockneys, in their delightfully smelly way, degraded the phrase by eroding the *g* from *flaming* and dropping the aitch from the word *horror*. Eventually *flamin'* and *'orror* collided and gave way to the second word becoming the imaginary noun *Nora*. It stuck and was soon joined by the preceding adjectives *bloody* and the more daring *fucking*.

......

From 'The Adventure Of The Fucking
Horrible Hatbox Collection.'

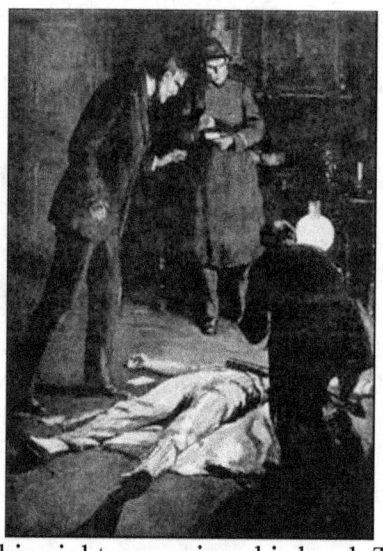

'Found dead in his nightwear minus his head. Tell me
constable, does he do this sort of thing often?' asked Holmes.
'Not to my knowledge, no,' replied the policeman.
'Seriously, you fucking answered that question? Oh my
fucking God.'

From 'The Filthy Fucking Knob Hound Of Hounslow.'

'You see, Watson, but you do not observe,' huffed Holmes.
'The woman in red clearly has bigger tits.'

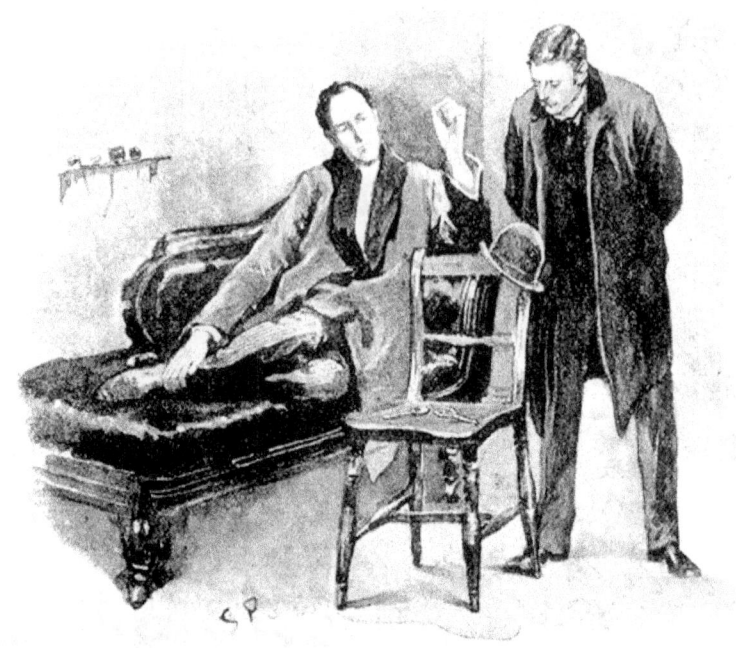

3. LADY SCATALO'S STOLEN BUM-NUGGET

'Really Holmes, have we the time to dilly dally over a silly hat?' protested Watson. 'This won't help us find perhaps the most expensive gemstone ever fashioned into the shape of a human plop.'

'On the contrary, Watson, the more we know of the wearer of this hat the quicker we can furnish Lady Scatalo with her precious Bum-Nugget. Now indulge me. What does this hat tell you about the intelligence of its owner?'

Watson puffed then gave the hat a long hard stare.

'Well, looking at it from a phrenological aspect, it's a large hat so the fellow must have a huge head, therefore a huge brain. It's definitely not big due to recent brain fever either, as the hat is old and worn. No, he's always been very clever,' offered Watson.

'Bravo!' laughed Holmes, clapping his hands.

'I got it right?' asked Watson beaming widely.

'No. You completely ballsed it up. The owner of this hat is a dozy shit for brains. Look outside, would you?'

Watson glanced outside to the rain-lashed Baker Street, then turned back to Swearlot, a look of blankness upon his visage.

Holmes snorted. 'It's pissing down outside and this thick bastard's forgotten his fucking hat.'

......

From 'The Sultan's Son & The
Arsehole Full Of Sheep's Eyes.'

'My apologies, Watson, a pipe in the eye might be deduction's poorer cousin but its results are much quicker. Just stop hiding my fucking drugs for God's sake.'

From 'The Adventure Of Spring Bollock'd Jack.'

" HOLMES WAS WORKING HARD OVER A CHEMICAL INVESTIGATION."

'Without a shadow of doubt, Watson, your Mary is dead.'
Watson gasped, 'But how?!'
'Kidding. I don't even know what all this crap does,'
chuckled Holmes.

The Adventure Of The Bladder Fairy

Pissy Reig, that foul scoundrel in the proportions of a toddler, has struck again. The middle aged anarchist in a child's body uses the breeze and her miniscule weight to float over picnics and garden parties to drop a golden shower on her victims.

Uncover the 3 differences in the draw-o-grams and we may yet stop the vile Bladder Fairy.

. . . . . .

4. THE ADVENTURE OF THE UNION JACK-ASS

Holmes perused the sketch book which contained page after page of drawings of the Union flag atop a myriad London establishments.

'And you say you've created a dozen similar books, Jericho? Each containing your own sketches of the Union flag?'

The clearly distraught American continued pacing the floor of 221*b for bastard* Baker Street, a look of dire anguish on his face.

'For sure, Mr Holmes. My business partner, Mr Dangler was adamant I document every single flag of your most noble capital. Why, I dunno know. We make farm tools.'

To the surprise of Holmes and Watson, Jericho threw himself to his knees, his hands raised pleadingly. 'Please Mr Holmes, I am surely going outa my mind with the strangeness of it all. I aint been back to America in months! What's it all mean?'

'It means you're a fucking idiot, sir. You have a younger wife, do you not? A pretty girl. Bit of a slut.'

'How on Earth did you know that?' gasped the American.

'You failed to blush when Mrs Hodsun took out her left tit and scratched it when she brought us the tea. You are a man used to the bawdiness of females. Your wedding band is garish and vulgar, obviously chosen by a woman. Women have no taste. Younger ones doubly so. Ergo you are married to a young, brash female. The fact she is pretty is proven by the fact your business partner is probably now, as we speak, up to his nuts in her guts whilst you are on a fool's errand drawing fucking flags in England.'

'You mean, he wanted me outa the way while he seduced my sweet Whoreena?' said Jericho, his bottom lip trembling.

'Frigging obvious, isn't it? Now send your partner a telegram saying you know what he's up to and when you get back you're going to kick seven shades of shit out of him,' Holmes ejaculated.

'I gotta admire your spunk, Mr Holmes, but I aint a violent man,' replied Jericho.

'Then become one, sir. In this life you are either the fucker or the fucked. Grow a pair of big boy's bollocks and show your rotten partner what a vindictive bastard you can be. Embezzle the company's funds, bankrupt the business and burn down the factory and his house. And if he's got a bird, bang the knockers off her.'

......

From 'The Astonishing Arse Biscuits of Lady Wiffington'

'Why yes sir, I *do* know the way to Marble Arch,' smiled the cabby amiably.
'Well fuck off there then!' laughed Holmes. 'Ha! Got another one, Watson'

SWEARLOT HOLMES

THE ADVENTURE
OF THE
FUCKING BIG LION

From 'The Disappearance Of Jock McCaber – The Cock
Mess Monster.'

After an awkward silence Holmes said, 'We'll go for a stroll,
you finish your wank, and then we can talk.'

5. THE MOIST SINGULAR HIDING PLACE OF MISS WINSUM

Watson was pensive. 'We can only assume the prophylactic is still within Miss Winsum, Holmes, so the sooner we get to her the better. Blast this train, can it not go any faster!'

'Fuck that, Watson, I did my dare, now it's your turn!' said Holmes, a twinkling of mischief in his austere, grey eyes.

Watson replied, 'Holmes, we have no time to play scary dareys! Retrieving the evidence and saving Lord Titmouse's honour is of paramount importance! Get a grip man!'

Holmes sneered and said, 'Yellow belly custard. I did mine. If you go into the train's toilets and you'll find the loo stuffed with bog paper and my widdle all over the floor. Now it's your turn!'

The consulting detective sat back and folded his arms defiantly.

Watson looked angered. 'Holmes, I must protest!' he snapped.

By now Holmes was on his feet flapping his folded arms like wings and making chick chick chicken noises.

Watson closed his eyes in desperation for a second. He took a heavy breath, realising capitulation to be his only remaining avenue. Tutting to himself, Watson reached up for the Emergency Stop handle.

......

From 'The Adventure Of The Rare As Fuck Bible.'

Holmes said, 'I assure you, Reverend, we will find your missing bible for this is a house of purity and God fearing morals.'
'Mr Holmes,' yelled Mrs Hodson from downstairs, her voice slurred by gin, 'Come and see the biggest turd in the world before I flush it. It's fucking huge!'
After an awkward silence the Reverend said, 'Please can I see the poo as well?'

From 'The Adventure Of The China Town Twats.'

Holmes sighed sarcastically and said, 'Here's what I wrote. Chicken chow mein, fried rice, _prawn crackers_ – oooh underlined!' He paused. 'So where's the fucking prawn crackers?'

From 'The Adventure Of The Senile Old Sod.'

'It is late and you are weary, Sir Charles. Here is a chair,' said
Holmes calmly, 'That I will wrap around your fucking head
unless you start being more cooperative.'

6. THE CURIOUS DAY FUCK ALL HAPPENED

It was a quiet afternoon in the rooms of 221*b for bastard* Baker Street. Both Holmes and Watson were engrossed in their newspapers, the silence broken only by the ticking of the mantelpiece clock and crackling of the fire.

'I see the Catholic Church has yet to choose a new head pontiff,' mused Watson, not looking up from his copy of The Times. 'Any idea who is in the running, old boy?'

After a pause, Holmes spoke. 'Several ideas, all of which I shall contemplate this very evening over a pipe or two of some fine Persian tobacco. Indeed, it may very well be a three pope problem.'

Both men remained looking at their papers as they chuckled with supressed dignity.

Another moment or two of silence fell then Holmes added, almost as an after thought, 'Rubbery yak's minge.'

Turning his page, Watson replied, 'Quite so.'

......

From 'The Shitty Squires Of Shoreditch.'

'You took your fucking time, Watson, you twat!' gurgled Holmes angrily! 'Shoot the bastards then!'

SWEARLOT HOLMES

A STUDY
IN
BEING FOUND DEAD
IN AN EFFEMINATE POSITION

From 'The Adventure Of The Band Of
Big Buttocked Bastards.'

'Why go all the way to the toilet compartment when there's
an open window to crap out of,' scoffed Holmes.

7. THE SHIT-HEADED CYCLIST PSYCHIATRIST

'So you think Professor Mesmer is behind these strange suicides, Holmes?' quizzed Watson. The detective ushered his finger to his lips, urging his friend to lower his voice.

In the dark alleyway behind Mesmer's practice, every sound echoed and Holmes wished their visit to be as quiet and as quick as possible.

'Makes sense, I suppose,' whispered Watson. 'Every one of the recent spate of suicides has been under hypnotherapy officiated by Mesmer. But how do we prove he hypnotised them into leaving all their worldly goods and chattels to him? I saw no evidence of opulence beyond his means. Did you?'

'Fuck that for the time being, Watson. I am more concerned with his slur upon me and my mother. Did you not hear him?' said Holmes as he undid the dust cap of the back tyre of Mesmser's bicycle. 'He said my compulsive swearing was probably a result of a pre-birth trauma. More likely that whilst I was in the womb, my mother came into contact with a foul-mouthed navvy. Probably an Irish one. Cheeky pseudo-science spouting shit-head. I'll fucking show him.'

With a whoosh the air from the second tyre raced out, rendering the bicycle unusable.

Suddenly there was the click of a lock from the back door of the practice. Holmes sprang to his feet and began running down the alley.

'Fucking leg it, Watson. The dirty bastard might hypnotise us and bum us!' said Holmes laughing excitedly.

Watson's eyes widened in horror. He clasped his hands against his posterior and took after his friend as fast as his legs would allow.

......

From 'The Adventure Of The Camp
Beasts Of Lord Woopsie.'

'Christ's tits, Watson, I said shoot the fucking thing, not
shag it!' growled Holmes, 'Bloody hell, if you want
something doing.'

From 'The Adventure of The Finsbury Flasher.'

'No Mr Flashman, this is not the floppy novelty you exposed to those distressed young ladies in the twilight,' replied Holmes. 'It was no dead goose, sir, but your own, very alive, cock!'

8. A FUCKING IDIOT IN DOWNING STREET

'Thank heavens you came, Mr Holmes,' puffed the flabbergasted junior minister Hetherington. 'The Prime Minister has gone totally mad this time. The entire cabinet is at a loss over what to do.'

Standing in the hallway of number 10 Downing Street, Swearlot Holmes and Dr Watson were handing their hats and coats to a servant girl with a lazy eye named Susan. What her good eye was called is of no consequence.

Holmes listened at the doorway of the conference room and could hear heavy stomping sounds and fierce growling.

'Does he have a wild animal in there with him?' questioned the consulting detective.

Sighing heavily, the junior minister said, 'No. That's his advisor, Operator Bowsfield, a brown bear that lives inside him. We'd better get in there as Bowsfield tends to smash ornaments when he's hungry.'

The three men burst into the room and Lord Ingleby Barwick was indeed in the posture of a bear and heading for the trophy cabinet. The minister rushed to stop him but in a trice Barwick was calm and adopted a normal stance.

'Thank you, Bowsfield, for your sage advice,' he said. 'Ah, Hetherington, prepare a memo. We have decided that from now on the human bottom is a sentient individual and entitled to its say. Bowsfield realised it. Clever bear that.'

Holmes interjected with a smirk on his face. 'Sir, are you saying bottoms will have their say in Parliament? Perhaps even have the vote?'

'Indeed yes,' snapped Barwick. 'Why, my bum is called Teacroft Davenport and he's very vocal about matters agricultural.'

The Prime Minister lifted his leg and let rip an enormously loud fart.

'Quite so, Davenport, farmers should get tax breaks. Make a note, Hetherington.'

Watson gasped and whispered to Holmes. 'He's a complete ga-ga-chumper, Holmes. I shall have him certified forthwith.'

'Eat shit and die, Watson,' laughed the detective as he turned to leave. 'Every politician since governments began has talked out of his arsehole, at least this mad bastard's being honest about it. Come on, let's fuck off.'

......

A Four Letter Cuss-Code

Fuck, tits, wank, dong, sods, crap, ring, cock, piss, shit.

Mary, Watson's tart, has been kidnapped. Her whereabouts are a mystery, but she's not your average shit for brains filly. She has sent us a Four Letter Cuss Code on a coffee shop napkin and the number sequence to crack it too.

Using the expletives and the numbers strictly in the order they have been written, take the corresponding letter from each cuss to form a new word to reveal where the fat cow is being held. To start you off the 4th letter of *fuck* is K.

CODE : 4 2 3 4 1 1 1 2 3 1

Write the answer to Mary's whereabouts in the space below letter by letter.

From 'The Adventure of The Twatty Thames Terrorist.'

'Run!' yelled Holmes, 'Run for your lives!'
'What is it, old boy? Another dire contraption of the Thames
Terrorist?' pleaded Watson.
'The biggest fucking spider in the world! Bastard looked right
at me!'

From 'The Honourable Lady And The Filthy Old Cow.'

'Please excuse Watson, Lady Carter,' implored Holmes, 'If brains were dynamite he would scarcely have enough to blow his fucking hat off.'

9. THE PISSED PARASITES OF SOBRIETY HALL

'It's as I suspected, Watson,' yelled Holmes as he tipped over the glass tank where the sleeping mosquitos were situated. It smashed with a tremendous noise, but none of the tragic alcoholics strapped to the beds even stirred.

The foul-mouthed detective stamped the wretched life out of each and every ecto-parasite so it could inflict no more wretchedness to human lives. He spoke as he worked.

'Reverend Shadrack has trained these little bastards to drink from these comatose alcoholics. Remember yesterday, we observed him injecting these tragic fuckers with something. I now know it is in fact a high octane alcohol and salt water solution. He then sets them onto members of his Temperance group, but instead of sucking blood up through their proboscis, the salt water causes the mosquitos to vomit the alcohol already inside them into their victims, rendering them pissed as farts. It's ingenious but the pious parson's hubris is doomed.'

Holmes eyed the debris carefully for a moment to ensure every single mosquito was dispatched.

'Whilst bladdered, the Reverend gets them to sign over their entire fortunes to him before they pass out. When they come round, they remember nothing of it, but are a good deal poorer. The scurrilous twat.'

To his shock, Holmes felt two arms clinch him around his waist. They were that of his colleague Watson.

'You're a very attractive fellow, Holmes, have I ever told you that?' said Watson with a slurred schoolgirl giggle.

'What the blue rinsed fuck?!' yelled Holmes. His eagle eyes immediately honed in on the mosquito embedded into Watson's neck.

Watson was off his tits too! With lightning precision Holmes took hold of the parasite by its wings, tore it from Watson's flesh and held it aloft. He then took up the riding crop and did smite it with such accuracy the malodorous creature was rent in twain.

Holmes turned to Watson who had by now climbed into bed with one of the alcoholics and fallen asleep. Thinking for a second, Holmes looked furtively around the room. He was the only one awake. He quickly took Watson's wallet out of his inside pocket, removed the ten one guinea notes, pocketed them and threw the wallet in the face of his snoring friend with tremendous force.

'Fucking molly,' said Swearlot as he ran out of the hall faster than shit off a hot, shiny shovel.

......

Professor Morifarty's
A Brief History
Of Swearing

'Minced Oaths'

The etymology of this particular mode of sweary-mary is far more sinister than you might imagine, heretically speaking. A minced oath is a way of saying something shocking without saying something shocking. Gadzooks, for example, is a *minced oath* based on the blasphemous *God's Hooks* - meaning the nails that secured Christ to the cross. *Gorblimey* means *God Blind Me*. Did you know, if a man utters a minced oath in a house of God his bollocks explode. If a lady does she becomes a lesbian.

......

From 'The Adventure Of The Indian, The
Italian And The Chinky.'

'Aha! Got one. The Maharaja Tandoori. They're still open,
but they don't deliver,' said Holmes, 'Watson, get your
fucking coat.'

From 'The Adventure Of The Indian, The Italian And The Chinky.'

'Yes it is rather a large Chinese takeaway for just one person, Watson,' said Holmes. He smiled. 'Look, I don't want to see my best friend hungry, so fuck off to another room will you.'

10. THE ADVENTURE OF THE PIMLICO PEEPING TOM

Holmes brought down the business end of his shooting stick across the back of Crompton's head and the vile peeping tom fell limp to the floor. Watson emerged from his hiding place in the empty house and said, 'Bravo Holmes. That'll teach the twisted blighter to spy on an innocent woman.'

Watson glanced out of the window across the street to the bedroom of Lady Fulsomrack and observed her entering her boudoir undressing herself.

'Take the dirty wrong-bollocks by the ankles and drag him downstairs, Watson. The Police have a paddy wagon waiting for the sick bastard.'

The good Doctor took Crompton's ankles in his hands and prepared to take the scurrilous rogue away to justice.

Watson said, 'He'll be bottom-bothered to death in Broadmoor and rightly so.'

'Why the screaming blue shittery would any man waste his precious time ogling something so banal as a woman,' mused Holmes. 'I've no explanation for it.'

His attention was captured by what Lady Fulsomrack was now doing. She was stood in full view of her open window without clothing and massaging her ample bosom with both hands.

'I mean, what is she doing now, for fuck's sake?'

Watson too glanced over and said, 'Oh they all do that before bed, Holmes. They rub pelican oil into their bosoms to keep them pert. She'll then place a thick candle between her breasts and rub them up and down vigorously to keep her cleavage healthy. My Mary does it. Vanity, I suppose. I leave her to it.'

Holmes looked distracted and somewhat puzzled. 'In full view of the window?' he asked, his voice now soft and wavering.

'Oh yes, something to do with the light of the moon keeping the nipples strong, I fancy.'

'I think I fancy her too,' stammered Holmes as he began to undo his britches.

'You okay, old boy?' asked Watson. 'Indigestion?'

'Yeah yeah. Go on, off you fuck. I'll erm... make sure Crompton had no accomplices.'

Watson departed the room dragging the Pimlico Peeping Tom behind him, the fiend's head rattling over every step on the staircase. As he left, he wondered if Holmes might be suffering an attack of asthma judging by the huffing and puffing noises he was making.

......

From 'The Adventure Of The Cold Turkey Detective.'

'The law cannot punish you but I can! Have an industrial strength Chinese Burn you fucking bitch whore!' growled Swearlot.

'Holmes, for pity's sake, she only forgot the sugar!' pleaded Watson.

SWEARLOT HOLMES

THE ADVENTURE
OF THE
PISSED STUDENTS

From 'The Adventure Of The Vexing
Velocipede Plundering Prick.

'When you have eliminated the impossible, whatever remains,
however improbable, must be the larcenist who stole my bike,' said
Holmes sagely. He looked up from their hiding place and gasped.
'That's the fucker! I'll kick his ghoulies up his dirty arse!'

11. A FOUL-MOUTHED COW IN BELGRAVIA

'Ha!' laughed Swearlot Holmes as he practically leapt from the Hansom Cab to the doorstep of 221*b for bastard* Baker Street where Dr John Watson stood awaiting him. 'I've beaten the shitty bitch!'

Holmes regaled his friend with the night's accomplishments, of how he tricked his way into Miss Stradler's house and located her secret hiding place. He'd even widdled in her underwear drawer just to add to her vexation. Tomorrow, Holmes would return with the King and retrieve the incriminating photograph showing her inserting a chimp into his Highness. Case closed.

A figure emerged from the foggy evening. A small man, from what could be gleaned of him in the dimness. He seemed to almost deliberately swerve into Holmes, barging him into Watson before walking on.

As he did, in an effeminate voice, he said, 'Good night, Mr Sharecock Homo, you repugnant, fuck faced pigmy's cock.'

And then he was gone.

'What a foul mouthed chap,' blustered Watson. 'And his expletives are worthy of yours.'

Holmes emitted a deject sigh.

'No, my friend, not worthy of, better than. That was Miss Stradler and I do believe she has beaten me.'

Irene Stradler was many things, a racist seamstress, a topless train driver, a human Moses basket for men in nappies and an exponent of sexual animal cruelty, but to Swearlot Holmes, she will always be 'That Fucking Woman'.

......

From 'Swearlot Fackin' Holmes Does The
Fackin' Knowledge.'

'Why do they call them Hansom cabs, Watson, when all the
drivers are all such ugly bastards?' mused Holmes.

From 'The Man With the Twisted Ball-Sack.'

'Oy you, you posh knob, wanker shithead,' sneered the grizzled old cockney tramp.
Watson sighed, 'Holmes I know it's you. I helped you apply that disguise not an hour ago.'

From 'The Adventure Of The Swearing Men.'

'But Mr Holmes, what can this cryptic message mean?' asked the Countess.
'Are you taking the piss?' replied Swearlot.

The Adventure Of Lord Claude Balls

Lord Claude's cat Celeste has been clamped onto his knacker sack for 3 weeks now and shows no sign of decamping said area. Swearlot's idea to remove the bollock bothering feline is

to shove a lit cigarette up it's furry arsehole. That'd shift the fucker. But, Lord Claude is hearing none of it as he mollycoddles the beast. Find the 5 subtle differences in the pict-o-etches to cease his Lordship's testicular tribulations.

. . . . . .

12. THE DIRE DESPERATION OF ANGUS McFADGIE

Holmes' disembodied voice was entirely audible but Watson could no more fathom from where it was coming than he could see the hiding detective.

'Confound you, Holmes, we do not have time for hide and seek! A young man's life is in the balance. We must get this fresh evidence to Pentonville Prison immediately lest the innocent Angus McFadgie will hang.'

Watson grabbed the mantelpiece clock and held to every corner of the room.

'It is nearly 7am. The execution is at 8 sharp.'

'Which means we have an hour to play, Watson. Now stop being a wanker and find me,' said Holmes.

Again, his voice seemed to come from nowhere and everywhere.

Watson ran around the apartments of 221*b for bastard* Baker Street looking under beds, in cupboards and behind furniture. He was frantic.

'Oooh freezing cold, old boy. So cold your cock's snapped off like a little icicle,' chuckled the swearing detective.

Watson ran back into the sitting room and yelled, 'Swearlot Holmes, stop this nonsense at once! I promised McFadgie we would save him from the gallows and we now have the proof he could not have poisoned her. The cyanide was administered early in the morning and no Scotsman is ever awake at this time, they're all sleeping off their drunken excesses of the night before.'

'D'er, I know, dick face. I worked it out by spending the evening observing the drinking routines of Scotsmen. It's deeply depressing so I want to play. Or are you saying you give up?' said Holmes.

'Yes!' shouted Watson! 'I give up, now will you please reveal yourself so we can get to the prison!'

'Bigguns,' laughed Holmes. And with that little Willy Bigguns walked in dressed as a bell boy, and a proper twat he looked too. He casually pulled back a curtain that revealed Holmes sat in a recess into the wall that Watson had never seen before.

Holmes said, 'I had this made whilst you were away fannying about with your quackery practice. It's exactly at a focal point juxtaposed to the acoustics of the entire building making it an ideal place to hide yet still speak without ever giving away your location.'

Bigguns suddenly clicked his fingers and stomped on the floor.

'What is it, Bigguns?' asked Holmes. 'And you look a proper twat, by the way.'

'Lummy guv, I've only gone and forgot to put all the clocks forward, Mr Holmes. It's British summertime, innit. Kwoar blimey, I'm a lame duck and no mistake. Apples and pears, do what and jellied eels.'

The mantelpiece clock, still in the hands of Watson, struck 7. Watson's throat went dry and he croaked, 'That means it's actually 8 o'clock.'

There was a very long and arduous pause as both men processed the information. It was broken when Holmes said, 'Oh fucking hell, McFadgie is, right now, dangling like a leg of mutton in a butcher's shop window. Shit, we've fucked up big style.'

Watson was trembling. He fell backwards onto the settee. Another moment passed.

'1, 2, 3, 4, 5,' said Holmes, his hands now covering his eyes.

Watson's mouth fell open. An innocent man had just been wrongly hanged and Holmes was *still* playing hide and seek. Watson thought for a moment but when Holmes reached 15, the Doctor sprang to his feet and ran off to hide.

'Coming ready or not!' shouted Holmes. He flicked Bigguns' ear and said, 'Sort those fucking clocks out, bell end boy.'

......

From 'Swearlot Holmes In Wonderland.'

'Pull yourself together, Holmes,' implored Watson, 'Your brain is addled by opium, man!'
'Watson, I saw a white rabbit and I'm following it!' snarled Holmes, 'I'm going to catch it, fuck it and kill it.'

From 'The Sinful Second Income Of The Rampant
Old Housekeeper.'

'Gerroff me y'fucking wankers!' wailed Mrs Hodson. Holmes
clapped his hands with glee. Seeing Mrs Hodson drunk was
more of a tonic than opium to the great detective.

From 'The Adventure Of The Fucking Gross Bitch.'

'Watson, this is a woman with a manky eye named Lady Brisket. What her good eye is called I have no fucking clue,' said Holmes.

13. THE RETURN OF THE GOLDEN MUMMY'S TITS

'It beggars belief, Mr Holmes. We have had break-ins here at the British Museum on several occasions, but something was always taken,' said Lord Rumbold.

'Yet on no occasion has your entire collection been intact after an intrusion, until now,' replied Holmes. 'Nothing was taken. Most perplexing.'

All assembled in the Museum offices pondered the previous night's events for a moment.

Then Lady Rumbold interjected by saying, 'I think we are looking for a left-handed intruder. The foot indentations in the grass by the broken window were slightly deeper on the right side. Ergo the villain was carrying something heavy under his right arm leaving his left free to work with. Gentlemen, we should not be looking for what is missing, we should seek out what is in the museum that was not here before the break-in.'

Holmes, Watson, Inspector Leturd and Rumbold looked at her with disgust and disdain.

'Get out,' seethed Rumbold. 'Go to the kitchen and await me there whence I shall cut off all your hair, you ridiculous harridan.'

Silently, Lady Rumbold rose and left the room.

'She must be having a period or a baby,' said Watson. 'They suffer brain fever at times like that.'

'My apologies, Mr Holmes. She won't be so loquacious with a blade one skinhead,' offered Rumbold.

'No no no,' laughed Swearlot. 'Not necessary. A bitch slap will suffice. Besides, whilst the daft cow was rabbiting on. I had time to think. I think we are looking for a left-handed intruder. The foot indentations in the grass by the broken window were slightly deeper on the right side. Ergo the villain was carrying something heavy under his right arm leaving his left free to work with. Gentlemen, we should not be looking for what is missing, we should seek out what is in the museum that was not here before the break-in.'

The men gasped with wide-eyed amazement and began clapping.

'Bravo, Holmes,' said Watson.

'I'm flabbergasted,' said Rumbold. 'How does he do it?!'

'I wish I had your insight, Mr Holmes,' offered Inspector Leturd.

'Aw, it was fuck all really,' laughed Holmes dismissively.

......

From 'The Fetid Mephitis Tipped Cigarollos Of Cairo.'

'Oh do stop being such a colossal male hairdresser, Watson,' smirked Holmes. 'By infecting you with the poison I can be sure you will use your last ten minutes devising the antidote. Necessity is the mother of invention and all that shite.'

From 'The Adventure Of The Flattened Corpse.'

Holmes was annoyed by her reluctance. 'Mrs Hagfish, please slam the frigging door against the wall. How else can I prove to you the fragility of the human body. The boy has been amply paid.'

14. THE ADVENTURE OF THE SUSSEX SWEARWOLF

Watson screamed and covered his ears. Inspector Leturd threw himself to the wet ground so his eyes would not burn out seeing the terrible blue beast. It snarled and growled in its thrashing before letting forth another archaic utterance of filth.

In a raspy dog voice it yelled, 'Mirkin stubble!'

Watson turned to flee, shouting, 'I cannot hear another swearword from that blasphemous devil dog!'

'Pull your cocking self together, Watson!' yelled Holmes. 'It's not a Swearwolf, it's just a fucking big dog!'

Leturd was fraught with terror.

He bellowed, 'But look, Holmes, it's ghostly profanities are turning the very air blue with supernatural iniquity!'

'Some sod's painted a bloody dog with luminous dye and taught it a few medieval swear words! Nothing more!' snapped Holmes, taking his Derringer pistol from his pocket.

'Arse-quake!' woofed the hound. 'Spunky stumps!'

'I'm the only one worthy to swear like an Australian woman, you furry fucker!' bellowed Holmes with studied anger. He fired, hitting the savage monster in the hind leg.

'Ow! You twatapus!' wailed the animal. It rounded on its wounded limb and took off into the darkness and fog at speed.

'You two fannies can get up now, it's gone,' said Holmes.

'Let's hope it stays in Hell this time,' said Leturd, shivering. He crossed himself.

'Oh piss off, Leturd. Someone has meticulously trained that dog in the art of swearing just to put the fear of God into people and my money is on Lord Bastardville. The only question that remains is why?'

The air was now still save for the panting of the three men. Then a distant howl permeated the misty black night followed by a deep echoing cry of, 'Wangers, nadgers and hot pizzle!'

'Hmm,' mused Holmes, 'this is a most curious incident of a dog in the night-time.'

......

THE HUNT FOR
THE SUSSEX SWEARWOLF

Quick Watson, it's a race to find all 7 archaic expletives from
the grid opposite before that cussing devil dog the Sussex
Swearwolf barks them! Hurry, the fucking game is afoot, you
twat!

<u>Vintage obscenities to find :</u>

Judas Priest, Shyster, Odsbodkins, Turd, Fishwife, Pizzle, Scullion.

```
O M R J C W D I O O
N C M U J R E D R Y
O Y I D P I Z Z L E
I X G A T Q W V C R
L L Q S E U M D E Z
L B C P R O R T A O
U K I R C C S D D K
C Y T I E Y L S I L
S S E E H F B Q Q B
D J H S V O S F E H
G Y F T D O J E Z E
D H O K V H S B F S
E F I W H S I F G J
X N G X T Y T T H G
S H F D L Q K D C D
```

From 'The Return Of The Sussex Swearwolf.'

'One thing is quite apparent about this supposed
Bastardville hound,' mused Holmes, 'It's shit is a
bugger to get off one's shoes.'

From 'The Unprincipled Exploitation Of The Successful Character The Sussex Swearwolf.'

'Watson, I must introduce you to my friend Jack, second name Shit,' said Holmes, 'It's obvious you don't know him.'

15. THE WANKER DETECTIVE

Emerson gingerly entered the Swearlot's bedroom, eyeing all around for a trap. The frail, gaunt figure in the bed was barely recognisable as the once tall and sleek, foul-mouthed detective Swearlot Holmes. His breathing was weak and intermittent.

A dry sinister smile crept over Emerson's cruel features.

'So it is true. You really are at death's door, Holmes,' laughed Emerson. 'I hope it's not long before it opens fully to you.'

Holmes groaned raspingly and whispered, 'You blinking rotter, Emerson. You did this to me. You smelly... thing you.' He coughed weakly.

Emerson clapped his hands with glee. 'Blinking? Rotter? Ho ho, you've completely lost your power of salacious prurience haven't you! Oh happy day for the criminal classes! The end of Swearlot Holmes!'

'Just tell me how, Emerson? How you, possibly the worst flaming criminal in all of London, managed to kill Swearlot Holmes?' said the dying detective.

'The gum on the return envelope I sent you. It was tinged with hemlock and belladonna. I knew you couldn't resist sending me a foul tirade of abuse by post if I gave you half a chance. It's how I killed all those old ladies after swindling them out of their life savings too. Quite brilliant am I not?'

'Actually you're a fucking dick-nose fanny scab,' quipped Holmes as he sprang cat-like from the bed! 'Watson, Leturd!'

Inspector Leturd and Watson burst from the wardrobe, stripped to the waist. A young policeman appeared at Holmes' bedroom door preventing the shocked Emerson from escaping.

'Nick the shitty bitch, Leturd.'

The Inspector clasped handcuffs onto Emerson's wrists.

Holmes squared up to Emerson and said, 'Think I'm some sort of vicar-mouthed wanker do you, Emerson? I was ten steps ahead of you all the fucking way and now we have your full confession. Stich that.'

Holmes head-butted Emerson and the fiend fell to the floor, blood gushing from his nose. Holmes turned to Watson and Leturd.

'Why have you two got your top bollocks out? I hope it's not what I think it is.'

Watson and Leturd looked sheepish and both thought for a second.

Watson said, 'No, erm. It's very hot in there and we were uncomfortable. Isn't that right, Leturd?'

'Yes! No! Yes!' stumbled Leturd. 'I mean, erm, we saw a moth in there and were worried it might eat our shirts and erm...' His voice tailed off.

'Just take Emerson to the bobby boutique. I'm going to wash this make up off and puke my fucking guts up, you sick mollies.'

......

From 'The Adventure Of The Tits-Out Librarian.'

'Aha! Here it is : **wanker**. And instead of a
definition there's just a picture of you, Watson.'

From 'The Adventure Of The Fart Hatter.'

Holmes struggled but could not escape the rope bindings. Morifarty said, 'Once the miasma of my unique bowel guff is upon your crown, it permeates the scalp resulting in agonizing brain death.' The fiend broke wind into his hat and stepped towards the panicked detective.

Professor Morifarty's A Brief History Of Swearing

The 'V' Sign

During England's long skirmishes with France, and us kicking their arses at every opportunity, our bowmen became the target of their *'la colère effiminate petulant.'*

If ever captured the French would chop off the English bowman's first two fingers to prevent him from ever firing another bow and arrow again. So, flashing one's intact fingers became a sign of defiance against bullies. A way of saying *'Up yours'*, *'You won't beat me'* and *'Am I scared? Am I fuck.'*

......

Find _Your_ Swearlot Holmes Insult

This is how the great swearing detective would describe you!
Imagine that! Pick one entry from the three lists and write them in
the box provided on the next page!

FIRST LETTER OF YOUR FIRST NAME :

A = Shite smearing
B = Overbearingly flatulent
C = Morally challenged
D = Blitheringly banal
E = Horrible Catholic
F = Nouveau riche
G = Fuck fuckerty fucking
H = Bilious & repugnant
I = Shitfaced & bombastic
J = Inept witch-finding
K = Flabby fish smelling
L = Criminally ugly
M = Seeping arsehole
N = Buttock rattling
O = Wankily disagreeable
P = Unintelligently fat
Q = Painfully viewable
R = Mentally disfigured
S = Nefariously geared
T = Revoltingly shuddersome
U = Intellectually threadbare
V = Wretchedly loud
W = Seedily unkempt
X = Malodorously putrid
Y = Inexpertly constructed
Z = Fartily stolid

THE MONTH YOU WERE BORN IN :
January = Mole gobbling
February = Reliably treacherous
March = Fucktardly
April = Sloth bumming
May = Unpunctually morose
June = Third nipple wearing
July = Googly eyed
August = Dangly bollocked
September = Toadying & sickening
October = Lumpy muffin topped
November = Irish navvy
December = Self harming

PICK A NUMBER :
1 = Stump botherer
2 = Mirkin breath
3 = Hangman's prick boil
4 = Male hairdresser
5 = Tuppence ha'penny whore
6 = Fucking fucker
7 = Sailor fancier
8 = Rambunctious shirt lifter
9 = Wanky bastard
10 = V.D. scab

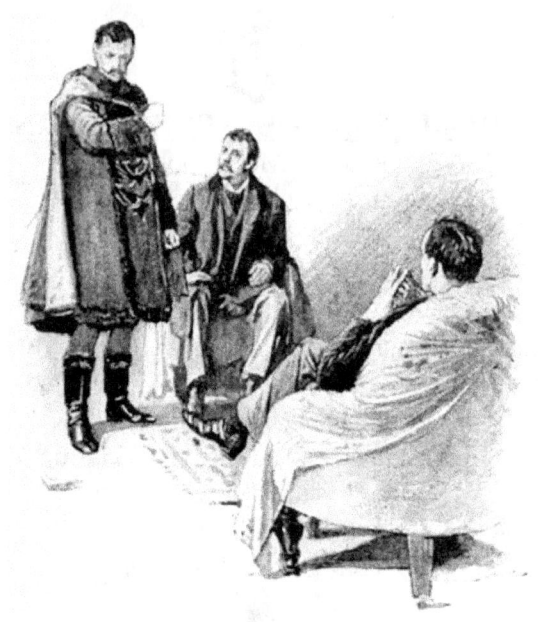

16. THE MISADVENTURE OF THE INSUFFERABLE SUFFRAGETTES

'I take it George Le Tiddler is not your real name,' asked Holmes as the male stripper dropped his britches.

'No, Mr Holmes, it's George Big-Penis, Le Tiddler is a stage affectation,' said the young man. He gestured to his bushy pubis and distinct lack of genitalia. 'You see gentlemen, my meat and two veg are gone. And it's not just me. Nine of my male stripper colleagues are also bereft of their beef bayonets and sex spuds which is no mean feat considering we were all endowed like shire horses.'

'It's incredible,' remarked Watson. 'And you say this happened during your act and you felt no pain whatsoever?'

'Correct, sir. The usual frenzied pawing and groping from the booze-fuelled females. One minute I was performing for the Suffragette & Spinsters Club of Peckham, the next I was peckerless. I am at loss to explain.'

'Suffragettes?' exclaimed Holmes. 'Those Godless monsters. I might have known. I think I've found your wanger. Show me your arse this instant.'

The young man turn around and sure enough there was his prod-rod shoved deep into his own rectum. Using his pipe as a lever, Holmes wrenched the lofty skin flute out and it flopped flaccidly between his leg, the testicles popping out after it.

'Gorgeous,' said Watson in a dreamy tone. Both Swearlot and George briskly turned to the Doctor who quickly corrected himself. 'George is… the victim of a cruel prank, Holmes.'

'Ah, you too noticed the puncture wounds on his buttock and lobber, hey?'

'I did. No doubt some local sedative to numb all feeling in both areas so the goods could be packed without raising suspicion. But why would they do such a thing?' said Watson.

'They hate men, Watson. Simple as that. Those vile penis-envying grotesques want the vote, equality and something called an orgasm and will degrade every man jack of us until they get what they want. This is an attack on the male populace incarnate.'

'Then what can we do to fight back?' asked Watson.

'I have an ingenious plan to push back the evils of feminism 250 years. By the time I am finished we'll be burning those latent todger-dogers at the stake,' remarked Holmes sitting back in his seat and placing his pipe in his mouth. Then like a thunderbolt, he shot to his feet spitting the pipe out. Wiping frantically at his lips with both hands, he ran to the bathroom making frantic gurgling and retching noises where he proceeded to puke his guts up.

……

From 'The Understandable Dismemberment Of The Pedantic Telephonist Slag.'

"WELL, WE SHALL BE ROUND ABOUT SIX, DR. WATSON WILL COME WITH ME."

'No, I said B, I want to speak to Scotland Yard. B. B! Bloody B!' Holmes paused as he listened. 'For fuck's sake just put Leturd on you ridiculous cow!'

SWEARLOT HOLMES

THE ADVENTURE
OF THE
STARING HYPNOTIST
BASTARD

17. THE ADVENTURE OF THE BEARDED SQUIRE

The two men danced around one another in the bar of The Resplendent Face Fuzz, fists tightly bundled in the best traditions of the Marquess Of Queensbury rules.

'You have no jurisprudence here, London. I am Squire of Beardonia. The Lord himself granted me this title and gave me his own beard as a facial crown of power,' snarled Featherwick.

'No sir, he did not. You are a cad and a bully and in my own humble opinion a fucking daft bastard,' retorted Holmes as he swung a lightning rod punch to Featherwick's face pulling a handful of beard from it upon its retreat.

Featherwick was mortified by the pain and the indignity of the attack but had no time to protest. Holmes landed another punch and grab and another clump of beard fell to the bar floor.

The blows came fast and furious until such a time only the odd wisp of facial hair remained. The floor resembled that of a successful barber's shop.

Featherwick was incandescent with rage. He turned to view his red raw and bald countenance in the mirror across the bar. Words failed him and gasps took their place. He turned back to Holmes who was lighting his pipe.

'The game is over, Squire Featherwick. I have relieved you of the beard of God. The powers it bestowed upon you are diminished. You will release all the villagers you have imprisoned in your cellar for non-payment of Beard Bursary and Tash Tax,' said Holmes. 'Oh, and you can have this as a warning against further beard growth.'

Holmes' booted foot rose up and struck Featherwick in the bollocks with a resounding thud. He doubled over and fell to the floor, no air left in his body to cry out. Swearlot stepped over him to leave. Before departing he said, 'Oh and I think your tortoise is escaping.'

......

From 'The Adventure Of The Elephant In The Room.'

'This Watson? Oh, it's a present for your fat fucker of a wife Mary,' said Holmes, 'It's a £500 Greggs voucher. Might last her a week.'

From 'The Adventure Of The Dirty Foreign Waiter
And The Shit Thick Ladies.'

'Gin, hair dye, king size tub of Ben & Jerry's,' mused
Holmes,' Yes, it's Mrs Hodson's writing. Poor fucker's
been dumped again.'

The Adventure Of Le Cirque Méchant

Egad! Those swearing, flatulent little abominations of nature
have returned. The Nasty Circus escaped from a freak show

to spread panic amongst the decent classes with their bawdy songs and le petomane bowel antics. If you can spot 5 differences in the images we may halt their terrible act.

. . . . . .

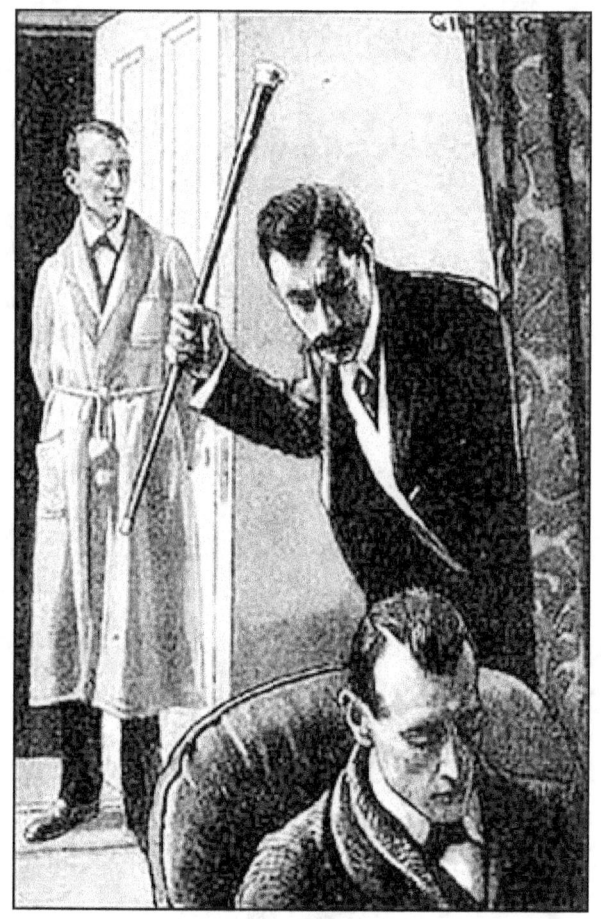

18. THE TERRIBLE MR TUPPENCE BOOTER

Swearlot flicked the V-sign at the back of his twin brother's head.

'I heard that, brother mine,' said Stately. 'Do not forget I too possess the power of expletives and I can recognise the swish of a V sign at forty paces.'

Quickly hiding his hands behind his back, Holmes said, 'And it is a power wasted upon you, to be sure.'

'I display the urbane decorum of a proper English gentleman and, as your elder by three minutes, demand you show the same.'

'If I had not sworn like a fucker in front of Lord Eggnog's wife she would never have become so pious he showed his true colours as a misogynist hater of women. Thus, I proved him to be the mysterious Tuppence Booter who has terrorised the good ladies of Mayfair by leaping from the shadows and kicking them in the quim.'

'Piousness will retain us the Empire, Swearlot. Also, Eggnog is still at large so you can't be that proficient at what you do.'

'He'll be caught within minutes, actually, prick boil.'

'Promise me you will desist your loutish, vulgar ways, little brother. Never again will you curse or act laddishly and most of all you will renounce your penchant for violence.'

Swearlot shrugged his shoulders and said, 'Then I promise just that,' and he stepped back into the darkness of his own bedroom.

There was a creak on the stairs and the sinister figure of Lord Eggnog appeared on the landing, a knobkerrie in his hand. Mistaking Stately for Swearlot, he raised it and brought it down on Stately's head. Before he could strike again, Holmes stepped out of his bedroom and crowned Eggnog with a cricket bat. So hard was the blow the bat split asunder and Eggnog was out for the count.

Rubbing his head in great pain, Stately furiously said, 'You knew he was coming didn't you!?'

'Of course. I saw him cross Baker Street a moment ago though the window.'

'And you knew he would mistake me for you! You could have easily stopped him, but you did not! Why?' growled Stately.

'You made me promise to renounce violence. I was following your lead.'

'But then you clocked him!' yelled Stately.

Swearlot produced his left hand from behind his back with crossed fingers. 'Ah yes, that's because not a second later I remembered I had had my fingers crossed when I made the promise, but by then it was too late. Sorry.'

'You fucking fetid colon full of stale shit you,' snarled Stately Holmes.

'Tut tut tut, you won't get into Heaven with a potty mouth like that, brother mine,' smirked Swearlot as he skipped downstairs to fetch the Pigs.

......

From 'The Adventure of The Wanker Bankers.'

'I'm glad we avoided Mycroft today, Watson, I owe
him twelve guineas,' said Holmes as they entered
the room. 'Aw fuck.'

From 'The Adventure Of The Visiting French Detectives.'

Holmes angrily leapt to his feet. 'Actually, detective work is 99% deduction and 1% handing out fucking big bitch slaps!'

19. THE ADVENTURE OF DAVEY JONES' COCKER.

Holmes was in the blackest of moods that Watson had ever seen him in. Treading on eggshells was an understatement when his disposition was this dire. The great swearing detective, whilst addled by inaction, was by his own admission a fucking pain in the arse.

'Your tea, Mr Holmes,' said Mrs Hodsun as she placed a silver tray of tea things on the table.

Holmes, hunched up in a chair, kicked out his leg and knocked over the table spilling the tea things everywhere.

'Oops a fucking daisy,' he sneered.

Ignoring him, she replied, 'And Inspector Leturd is here to see you. Shall I show him up?'

'Why not, you show me up just by being in the same pissing room, you old shit-stained haversack of hate,' said the petulant detective.

'Now now, Mr Holmes, no need for that,' said Leturd as he entered the room, a broad smile on his face. Hodsun left, shaking her head.

'Put weight on I see, Leturd,' said Holmes after a second's glance at him.

Inspector Leturd patted his stomach wryly. 'Maybe a pound or two.'

'A fucking stone or two, you fat bastard. Watson, get in here before Scotland Lard eats me. Watson!'

Dr Watson entered the room and sighed. 'Ignore him, Inspector. The man's an absolute nightmare when he has no case to occupy his attention.'

'Well then he'll be a delight today, Doctor, as I have a mystery that is as perplexing as any other. Fifteen sailors bummed to death, all in the same locked cabin,' said Leturd with gusto.

Holmes' eyes widened and he leapt to his feet. With child-like fascination in his voice he said, 'I'm liking this! Watson you could call it 'The Demon Of The Seamen' or 'The Adventure Of The Naughty Nautical Bottom Botherers'.

Watson winced politely and waved his head from side to side.

'Hmmm, let me do the writing up old boy.' Watson turned to Leturd and asked, 'These sailors, how handsome were they? Naked too, one would presume.'

Holmes was ecstatic by now and put his arm around the Inspector's waist.

'You must take me to this deliciously paradoxical locked cabin after the wonderful Mrs Hodsun has furnished us with some of her scintillatingly delicious tea. Sit down friend Leturd. Oooh, you've lost weight, haven't you.'

Like an excited child on Christmas morn, Swearlot Holmes clapped his hands together and giggled, 'Big fat pissy bollocks!'

......

SWEARLOT HOLMES

THE ADVENTURE
OF
LORD BOSTOCK'S
INVISIBLE MISTRESS

From 'A Study In Ass Gas.'

'Watson, don't think that by sitting over there I don't know you've farted three times in as many minutes,' sighed Homes, 'Eggy sod.' The detective suddenly straightened as an idea came to him.

From 'The Stradivarius Up The Arsehole And The
New Found Respect For Dr Watson.'

'Hmmm, so Watson's got a colossal headache today has he?
Well, let's see how loud this fucker can go?'

20. THE FINAL EXPLETIVE

'We meet at last, Swearlot,' said Morifarty amiably but with a distinct aspect of venom in his face. 'Forgive me, but I expected less of a dick-nosed, shit for brains devotee of pink feathered cock.'

'Obvious facial feature slur, intellect assassination quip, cheap remark regarding sexuality. It's fairly text book swearing, Morifarty,' replied Holmes looking out over the powerful gushing waterfalls of Switzerland's Shite-Ernbach Falls. He stepped closer to the edge of the abyss, the water roaring all around both men.

Morifarty's eyes narrowed and he stood level with Swearlot. 'A mere naughty aperitif before a sinful smorgasbord of blasphemous execration that would have the Marquis De Sade incandescent with blushes. One which will finish you forever, Swearlot. It's time to away with your jaded playground banter. A new order of diabolical cussing is upon us, you long streak of malodorous bladder funk.'

'Oh, you can up your game. I was beginning to surmise someone with the appellation Morifarty would not be able.'

Morifarty smiled. 'An unassuming moniker that lures those less salaciously gifted as ourselves into a false sense of security. Apt too seeing as I managed to trick you all the way to a place childishly called Shite-Ernbach for your last bow.'

The two aficionados of potty mouthing stood in silence for a moment as the waterfall roared on regardless.

'Swearlot! Swearlot!' came a voice behind them. Neither man turned for they had both pre-empted the arrival of Watson. The Doctor was running down the mountain path, his trusty service revolver in his hand.

'Join me, Swearlot. Imagine the politicians, the crowned heads of state, the great and the banally good we could insult. Why, within a matter of months we could have this drab world swearing with such bawdy coarseness it would be a utopia of indecency!' said Morifarty with genuine passion in his voice.

Swearlot could see the sincerity in his wicked eyes and appeared to contemplate it for a second.

'Nah, fuck off,' said Swearlot finally as he pushed Morifarty into the watery chasm.

Just as the flailing body of Morifarty disappeared into the powerful foaming torrents to be dashed to pieces upon the rocks within, one final profanity did he utter, barely audible above the deafening wash. A short, four letter word only Swearlot could make out with any clarity.

And he was gone.

Holmes stiffened, his eyes bulging. He now seemed speared with horror, addled by defeat.

Watson pulled an incredulous face. 'What did he say? Your ears are younger than mine, Swearlot. It was something like *runt* or *hunt*. What was it?'

For a moment Swearlot said nothing, then his face illuminated into the widest smile Watson had ever seen visited upon it.

'Nah, daft fucker probably shat his pink silk molly drawers. When you write this up you shall call it *His Last Shit*,' said Holmes.

Upon that, he turned on his heels and walked back up the mountain path with brisk vigour. Watson took one last look into the never-ceasing down surge of water.

Holmes shouted back to him, 'Come on then, lard arse. I'm so hungry I could eat a wanking monkey. Do these Swiss fuckers know how to make proper English chips then?'

•

SOLUTIONS

```
O   M   R   J   C   W   D   I   O   O   H
N   C   M   U   J   R   E   D   R   Y   O
O   Y   I   D   P   I   Z   Z   L   E   L
I   X   G   A   T   Q   W   V   C   R   M
L   L   Q   S   E   U   M   D   E   Z   C
L   B   C   P   R   O   R   T   A   O   S
U   K   I   R   C   C   S   D   D   K   I
C   Y   T   I   E   Y   L   S   I   L   S
S   S   E   E   H   F   B   Q   Q   B   A
D   J   H   S   V   O   S   F   E   H   B
G   Y   F   T   D   O   J   E   Z   E   I
D   H   O   K   V   H   S   B   F   S   G
E   F   I   W   H   S   I   F   G   J   T
X   N   G   X   T   Y   T   T   H   G   I
S   H   F   D   L   Q   K   D   C   D   T
```

The Adventure Of The Bladder Fairy

Extra hole in umbrella,
Handle inverted,
Legs missing,
Weird cloud knob in the sky,
The appearance of Gladstone.

The Adventure Of Lord Claude Balls

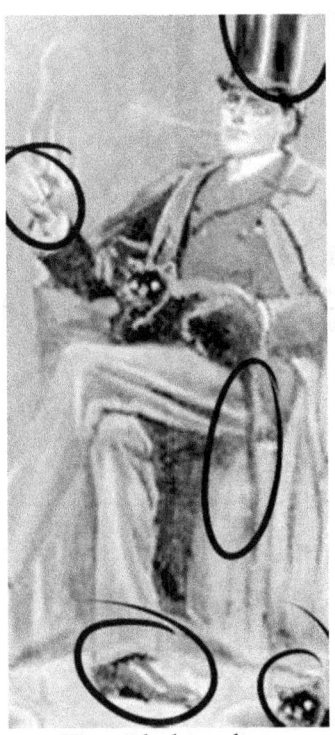

Extended top hat,
Hand aflame,
Celeste's elongated tail,
Spacky foot,
Extra Celeste.

The Adventure Of Le Cirque Méchant

Extra eye in Bertov's head,
Extended cane,
Drablo's inflated head,
Bit of the wall missing,
Tittybarp's extra leg.

…..

A Four Letter Cuss-Code

kings   cross

Read more from Dean Earle Wilkinson at
deanwilkinson.net

The Legend Of Arthur King,
Arthur King & The Curious Case Of The Time Train

The Classic Classic Children's Television Quiz Book

Disturbing Bedtime Tales (For Very Bad People) Ebook Only

SWEARLOT HOLMES – A STUDY IN SOCIAL NETWORKING

Your favourite swearing detective is on most of the top networking thingies. Twitter, Facebook, Tumblr to name but all of them. Tune in for regular updates on cases and shit.

Watson has announced his engagement to Miss Morstan. I am pondering how many shits not to give.

Have you ever noticed how Morifarty has a face like a bulldog licking piss off a nettle?

Got to collect Mrs Hodson from the cells. She got bladdered at bingo and kicked the fuck out of someone. Every Sunday night.

Watson's eaten the last of the corn flakes. Fucking fuckety fucktard! There's only coco-pops left. What the fuck am I, 7?

If this waiter asks me if I want a slice of lemon in my gin one more time I will insert a full one into his fucking arsehole. Lemon-entry.

Mrs Hodson has stunk the bog out. Again. Hate her.

Leturd's just slipped on a massive pile of horse shit in Baker Street! I nearly wet me bastard britches!

Leturd has admitted being out of his depth. I said 'Leturd you'd be out of your depth in a snake's piss.'

Consulting detective? Pah! I may as well be a gynecologist the amount of twats I have to deal with.

I'm starting to think I should fire Watson and employ a big, thick, pile of shit. Same difference.

The Red Headed League? Bunch of creepy ginog fuckers more like it. Horrible.

Watson wants to track the Hound Of The Bastardvilles. Fuck that. I'm not getting my arse bitten off for some posh twat.

Morifarty thinks he's the Napoleon of crime. Ha! The Napoleon of dickheads more like it. Arsehole.

Mrs Hodson's farted. What the fuck has she been eating?! It's like an invisible pea souper for the olfactory senses.

If Leturd thinks I'm cracking this case for him he can eat the Devil's shit biscuits.

The Baker Street irregulars have bought me a tie pin. Little fuckers made me cry. Love those smelly urchins.

Watson has just fallen down the stairs. Pissing myself laughing!

Also from MX Publishing

By Andrew Murray and Deakin Brook

Who's your favourite Sherlock Holmes? Benedict Cumberbatch or Rob Downey Jr.? Jonny Lee Miller or Jeremy Brett? It's so hard to choose, so spare a thought for poor Dr Watson – faced with so many Sherlocks old and new, what will he do? Who's so the wrong height? Who's too black and white? Who's too pale of face? Who's in the wrong place? Who's the right Sherlock in Doc Watson's view? And is Watson's Sherlock the Sherlock for you?

Also from MX Publishing

Who's your favourite Dr Watson? Martin Freeman or Jude Law? Lucy Liu or Edward Hardwicke? It's so hard to choose, so spare a thought for poor Sherlock Holmes - faced with so many Watsons old and new, what will he do? Who's too techno-garish? Who's too teddy-bearish? Who's maybe too pretty? Who's in the wrong city? Who's the right Watson in Holmes's own view? And is Sherlock's Watson the Watson for you?

Also from MX Publishing

A collection of hundreds of Sherlock Holmes puns amassed over decades and stolen from a host of sources. The wordplay may be familiar, but the settings and characters are all original to the sources cited. The puns that have made it into the book are all Sherlockian narratives. Each is a tale describing events featuring Holmes characters, not simply a comment or an observation. We warn traditional Holmes fans up front, you will be annoyed and offended. If you are not, then the authors simply have not found your particular hangup - yet. Pick a number, they will get to you in a later edition.

Also From MX Publishing

MX Publishing is the world's largest specialist Sherlock Holmes publisher, with over a hundred titles and fifty authors creating the latest in Sherlock Holmes fiction and non-fiction.

From traditional short stories and novels to travel guides and quiz books, MX Publishing cater for all Holmes fans.

The collection includes leading titles such as _Benedict Cumberbatch In Transition_ and _The Norwood Author_ which won the 2011 Howlett Award (Sherlock Holmes Book of the Year).

MX Publishing also has one of the largest communities of Holmes fans on Facebook with regular contributions from dozens of authors.

www.mxpublishing.com

Also from MX Publishing

Our bestselling short story collections 'Lost Stories of Sherlock Holmes', 'The Outstanding Mysteries of Sherlock Holmes', 'Untold Adventures of Sherlock Holmes' (and the sequel 'Studies in Legacy') and 'Sherlock Holmes in Pursuit'.

www.mxpublishing.com

Also From MX Publishing

London, 1920: Boston-bred Enoch Hale, working as a reporter for the Central Press Syndicate, arrives on the scene shortly after a music hall escape artist is found hanging from the ceiling in his dressing room. What at first appears to be a suicide turns out to be murder . . .

(the first in the Sherlock Holmes and Enoch Hale trilogy)

www.mxpublishing.com

Also from MX Publishing

Lego Sherlock Holmes

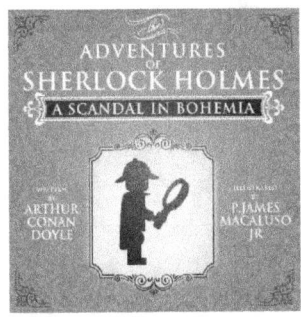 

Seven original adventures from Sir Arthur Conan Doyle, re-illustrated in Lego.

In this book series, the short stories comprising The Adventures of Sherlock Holmes have been amusingly illustrated using only Lego® brand minifigures and bricks. The illustrations recreate, through custom designed Lego models, the composition of the black and white drawings by Sidney Paget that accompanied the original publication of these adventures appearing in The Strand Magazine from July 1891 to June 1892.

www.mxpublishing.com

Also from MX Publishing

"Phil Growick's, 'The Secret Journal of Dr Watson', is an adventure which takes place in the latter part of Holmes and Watson's lives. They are entrusted by HM Government (although not officially) and the King no less to undertake a rescue mission to save the Romanovs, Russia's Royal family from a grisly end at the hand of the Bolsheviks. There is a wealth of detail in the story but not so much as would detract us from the enjoyment of the story. Espionage, counter-espionage, the ace of spies himself, double-agents, double-crossers...all these flit across the pages in a realistic and exciting way. All the characters are extremely well-drawn and Mr Growick, most importantly, does not falter with a very good ear for Holmesian dialogue indeed. Highly recommended. A five-star effort."
The Baker Street Society

www.mxpublishing.com

Also from MX Publishing

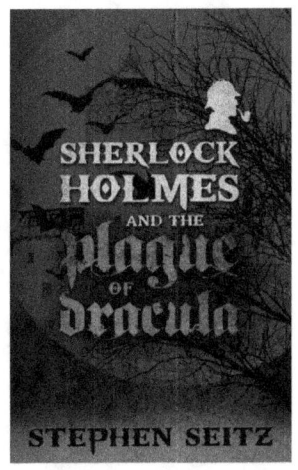

After Mina Murray asks Sherlock Holmes to locate her fiancee, Holmes and Watson travel to a land far eerier than the moors they had known when pursuing the Hound of the Baskervilles. The confrontation with Count Dracula threatens Holmes' health, his sanity, and his life. Will Holmes survive his battle with Count Dracula?

www.mxpublishing.com